Erica S. Perl   *Illustrated by* Arthur Howard

Goatilocks
and the
Three Bears

Beach Lane Books ❀ New York   London   Toronto   Sydney   New Delhi

For Roo, who is a gem—E. S. P.

BEACH LANE BOOKS

An imprint of Simon & Schuster Children's Publishing Division

1230 Avenue of the Americas, New York, New York 10020

Text copyright © 2014 by Erica S. Perl

Illustrations copyright © 2014 by Arthur Howard

BEACH LANE BOOKS is a trademark of Simon & Schuster, Inc.

For information about special discounts for bulk purchases, please contact Simon & Schuster
Special Sales at 1-866-506-1949 or business@simonandschuster.com.

The Simon & Schuster Speakers Bureau can bring authors to your live event. For more
information or to book an event, contact the Simon & Schuster Speakers Bureau at 1-866-248-3049
or visit our website at www.simonspeakers.com.

Book design by Sonia Chaghatzbanian and Irene Metaxatos

The text for this book is set in Grit Primer.

The illustrations for this book are rendered in watercolor.

Manufactured in China

0314 SCP

First Edition

10 9 8 7 6 5 4 3 2 1

Perl, Erica S.

Goatilocks and the three bears / Erica S. Perl ; illustrated by Arthur Howard.—First edition.

p. cm.

Summary: In this version of the classic tale, a hungry goat pays a visit to the home of the three
bears.

ISBN 978-1-4424-0168-6 (hardcover)

ISBN 978-1-4424-8989-9 (eBook)

[1. Folklore. 2. Bears—Folklore.] I. Howard, Arthur, illustrator. II. Goldilocks and the three bears.
English. III. Title.

PZ8.1.P42Go 2014

398.2—dc23

[E]

2012044918

Once upon a time, there was a kid named Goatilocks.

She lived down the road from a family of bears.

When the bears went out
for a walk one morning . . .

well, you can probably guess what Goatilocks did.

Inside the bears' house, Goatilocks
found three bowls of porridge.

She tasted the big bowl, but it was too hot.

She tasted the medium bowl, but it was too cold.

Then she tasted the little bowl. *Mmm!* It was just right. So . . .

she ate it.

(The little spoon, too.)

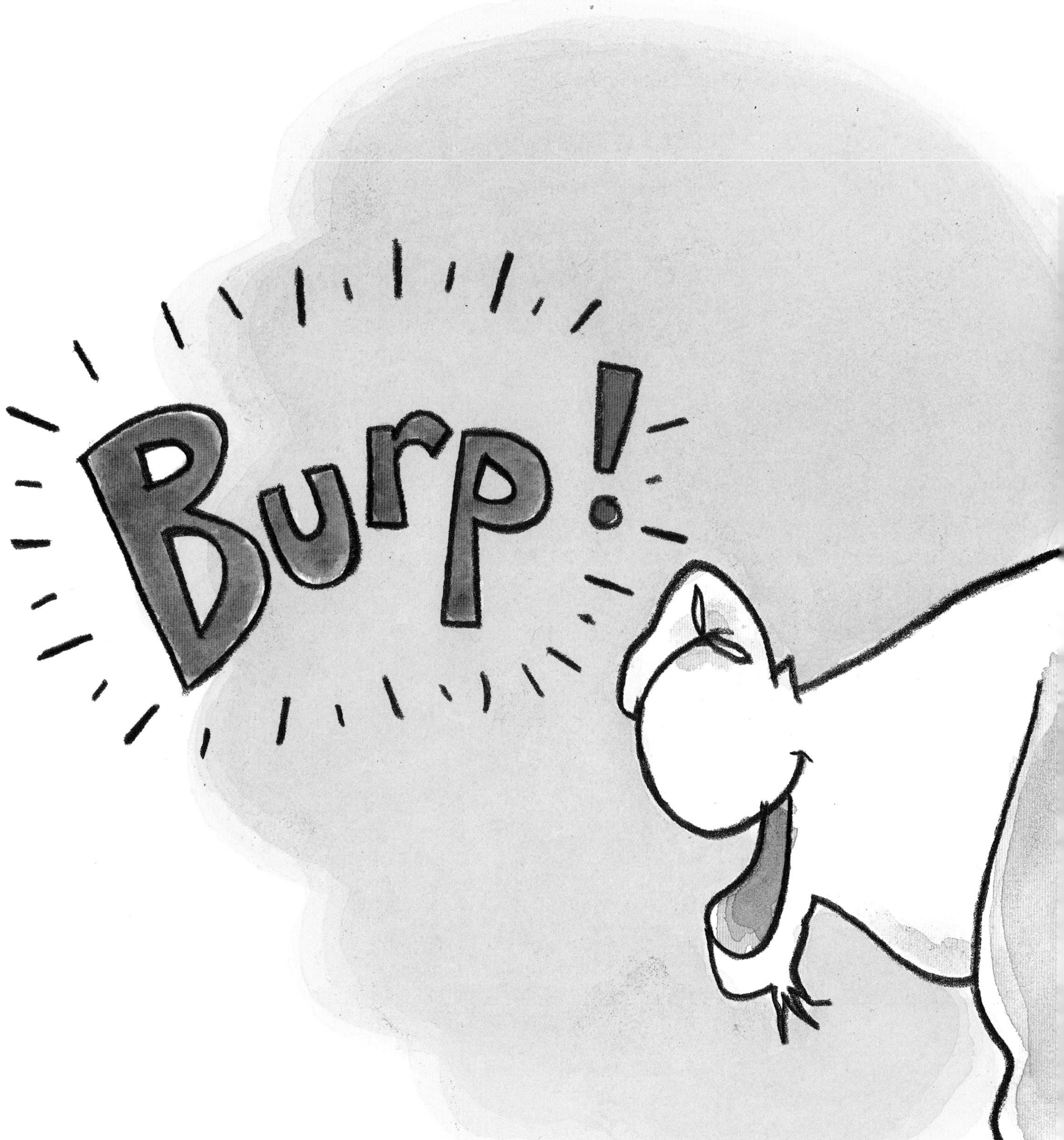
Burp!

Next, Goatilocks found three chairs.
She tried the big chair, but it was too hard.

She tried the medium chair, but it was too soft.

Then she tried the little chair. *Oooh!* It was just right. So . . .

she ate it.

(Cushions and all.)

At this point, Goatilocks began to feel sleepy.
Upstairs, she found three beds.
She tested the big bed, but it was too lumpy.

She tested the medium bed,
but it was too squishy.

Then she tested the little bed.
Ahhh! It was just right. So . . .

she ate it.

(Plus the blanket,
two pillows,
and a pair of
pajamas.)

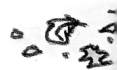

Then, with a contented sigh,
Goatilocks fell fast asleep.

Shortly thereafter, the bears came home.
You can probably imagine the commotion.

"Someone has been eating
my porridge," said Papa Bear.

"Someone has been eating
my porridge," said Mama Bear.

"Hey, where's my porridge?"
asked Baby Bear.

"Get a load of this!" called Papa Bear from the dining room. "Someone has been sitting in my chair."

"Gracious!" said Mama Bear.
"Someone has been sitting
in *my* chair."

"Hey, where's my chair?"
asked Baby Bear.

They found the culprit upstairs.
"My bed!" wailed Baby Bear. "It's . . . GONE!"
Goatilocks opened her eyes.

Above her stood three bears.

Quickly, she jumped up and hoofed it for home.
Which probably sounds like the end of the story.
But . . .

the next day, Goatilocks woke up
feeling a little, well, sheepish.
She wanted to make things right
with her neighbors. But how?

Outside, she found her answer.

How could the bears resist?
Her gift was so pretty.
So thoughtful.
It was just right.
So . . .

they ate it!